raising readers

Reading Together is Fun!

Children across Maine receive books from their doctors at each well child visit until they turn five. We hope your family has enjoyed reading them together.

Reading aloud to your child every day is important. Spending time reading to your child – even 20 minutes a day – is a wonderful gift!

There are lots of ways to have fun with books. Turn to the back of this book for ideas about activities your family can do together.

Raising Readers is a Maine health and literacy program funded by the Libra Foundation.

Visit us at: www.raisingreaders.org

Down by the Station

BY WILL HILLENBRAND

Harcourt, Inc.

ORLANDO   AUSTIN   NEW YORK   SAN DIEGO   LONDON

Library of Congress Cataloging-in-Publication Data
Hillenbrand, Will.
Down by the station/by Will Hillenbrand.
p. cm.
"Gulliver Books."
Summary: In this version of a familiar song,
baby animals ride to the children's zoo on the zoo train.
ISBN 978-0-15-201804-7
Special Markets ISBN 978-0-15-206651-2
1. Children's songs—Texts. [1. Zoo animals—Songs and
music. 2. Animals—Infancy—Songs and music. 3. Songs.]
I. Title.
PZ8.3.H553Do 1999
782.42—dc21
[E]   98-41770

Q P O N M L K J I H

Manufactured in China

The illustrations in this book were created in mixed media
on vellum, painted on both sides.
The display type was set in Belwe Bold Condensed.
The text type was set in Worcester Round Bold.
Color separations by Bright Arts Ltd., Hong Kong
Printed by South China Printing Company, Ltd., China
Production supervision by Stanley Redfern
Designed by Kaelin Chappell and Will Hillenbrand

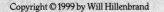

To Liz; Charlie;
my wife, Jane;
and my son, Ian

Down by the station
early in the morning.

See the little puffer-bellies
all in a row.

See the engine driver
pull his little lever. . . .

Puff, puff,
Toot, toot,
Off we go!

Down by the elephants
early in the morning.
See the little calf
waiting to go.
See the engine driver
pull his little lever. . . .

Puff, puff,
Toot, toot,
Thrump, thrump,
Off we go!

Down by the flamingos
early in the morning.
See the little chick
waiting to go.
See the engine driver
pull his little lever. . . .

Puff, puff,
Toot, toot,
Thrump, thrump,
Peep, peep,
Off we go!

Down by the pandas
early in the morning.
See the little cub
waiting to go.
See the engine driver
pull his little lever. . . .

Puff, puff,
Toot, toot,
Thrump, thrump,
Peep, peep,
Grump, grump,
Off we go!

Down by the tigers
early in the morning.
See the little cub
waiting to go.
See the engine driver
pull his little lever. . . .

Puff, puff,
Toot, toot,
Thrump, thrump,
Peep, peep,
Grump, grump,
Mew, mew,
Off we go!

Seal Island →

Down by the seals
early in the morning.
See the little pup
waiting to go.
See the engine driver
pull his little lever. . . .

Puff, puff,
Toot, toot,
Thrump, thrump,
Peep, peep,
Grump, grump,
Mew, mew,
Flip, flop . . .

DANGER

Uh-oh!

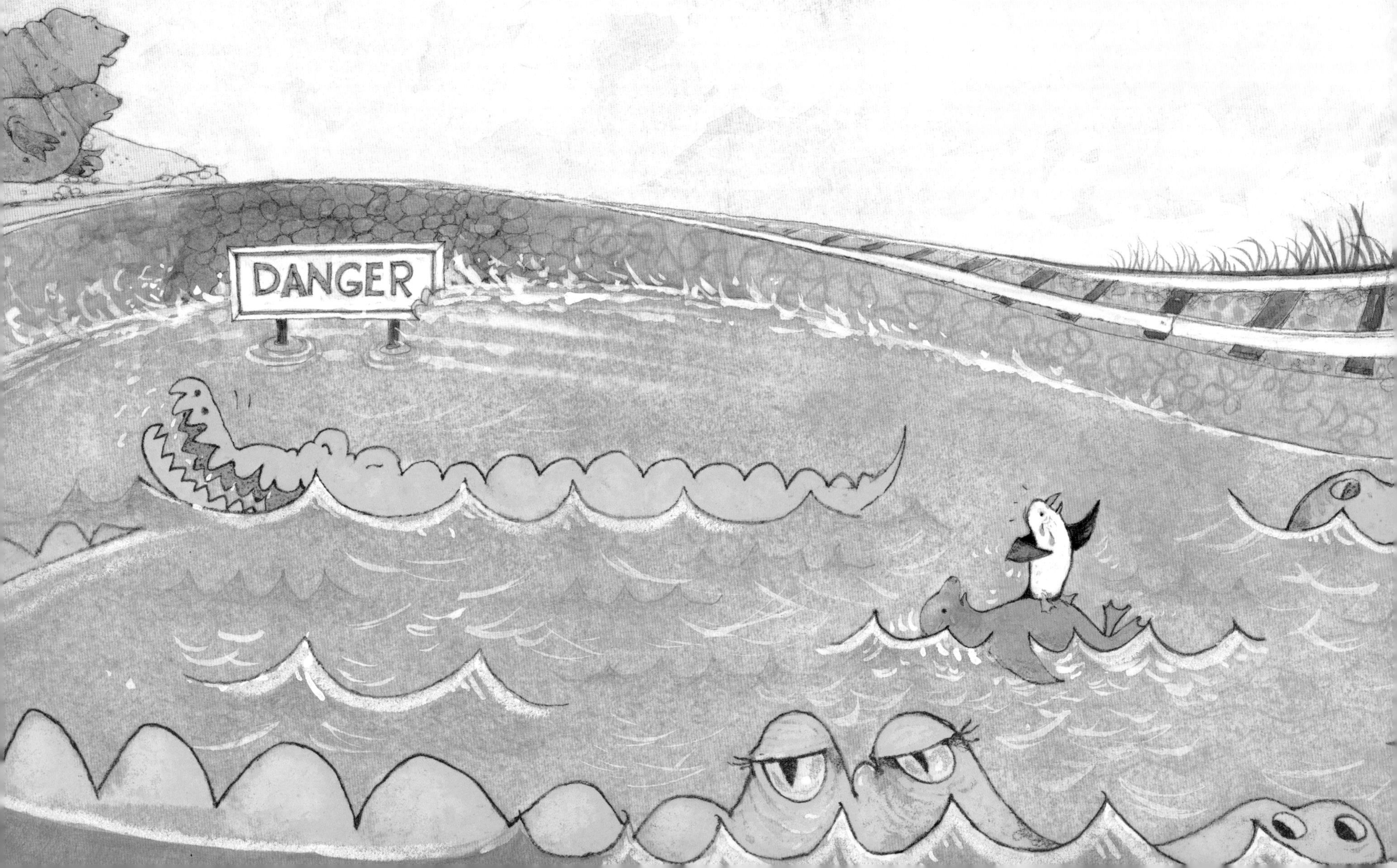

Phew!

Down by the kangaroos
early in the morning.
See the little joey
waiting to go.

See the engine driver
pull his little lever. . . .

Puff, puff,
Toot, toot,
Thrump, thrump,
Peep, peep,
Grump, grump,
Mew, mew,
Flip, flop,
Bump, bump,
Off we go!

Down by the children's zoo
early in the morning.
See the baby animals
exit in a row.
See the engine driver
pull his little lever. . . .

Puff, puff,
Toot, toot . . .

Off we go!

Down by the Station

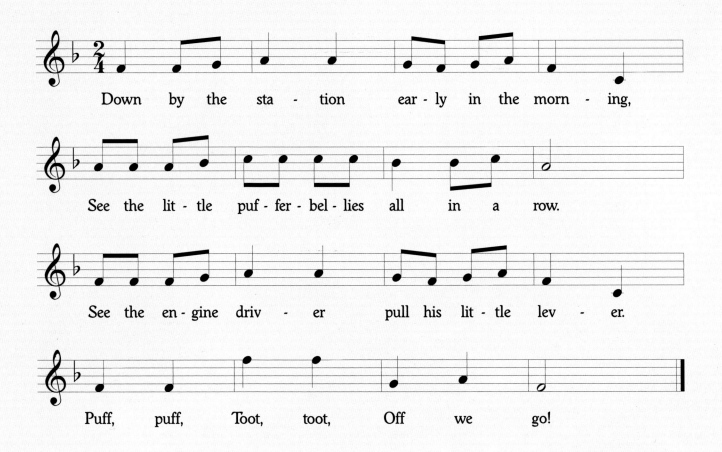

Additional Read Aloud Fun from Raising Readers

Children fall in love with books because of the memories created when they snuggle up and read with someone they love.

There are many ways to read a book with your child. Here are some ideas to help your child understand the story better, learn something new, or just laugh a little louder. Don't worry if some of the ideas below don't work for you – the most important thing is to enjoy the story together! Happy Reading!

SING THE SONG

"Down by the Station" is an old nursery rhyme that can be either read or sung. Why sing? It makes words more fun! Need help with the music? Listen to the song at www. raisingreaders.org or make it up!

You can also make music by having your child clap to the repeated sounds. Clap with your child on the words: "Puff, puff, Toot, toot, Peep, peep..." and so on. When kids use their hands while singing or reading it helps them feel like part of the story.

LOOK CLOSELY

The illustrator, Will Hillenbrand, has put many fun things in the pictures that are not in the words. For example, watch the monkey on every page. He has a story all his own. After reading the book a few times, ask your child to follow the monkey. Ask what the monkey is doing. You can repeat this for all the animals or other things in the book, like the red balloon.

Every book has hidden treasures. The biggest treasure, of course, is the time you spend with your child reading together.